MCR

MCR
AUG 2 3 2008

EVANSTON PUBLIC LIBRARY
W9-ANY-324

River Beds

Sleeping in the World's Rivers

By Gail Langer Karwoski
Illustrated by Connie McLennan

Publisher's Cataloging-In-Publication Data

Karwoski, Gail, 1949-
River beds : sleeping in the world's rivers / by Gail Langer Karwoski ; illustrated by Connie McLennan.

p. : col. ill., map ; cm.

Summary: In this sequel to Water Beds, readers go on an around-the-world boat ride to learn how mammals sleep in or around ten major rivers of the world. Includes “For Creative Minds” section with animal adaptation activities and a world map.

Interest age level: 004-009.
Interest grade level: P-4.
ISBN: 978-0-9777423-4-9 (hardcover)
ISBN: 978-1-934359-31-0 (pbk.)

1. Stream animals--Juvenile literature. 2. Rivers--Juvenile literature.
3. Sleep behavior in animals--Juvenile literature. 4. Stream animals.
5. Animals--Sleep behavior. 6. Rivers. I. McLennan, Connie II. Title.

QL145 .K36 2008
591.76/4 2008920387

Printed in China

Sylvan Dell Publishing
976 Houston Northcutt Blvd., Suite 3
Mt. Pleasant, SC 29464

To Laurence Pringle: mentor, inspiration, and friend—GK
To Jessica—CM

Thanks to all the many scientists and educators from zoos, aquariums, conservation, and research organizations for verifying the accuracy of the information in this book:

River Otters: Kelly Reno, River Otter Animal Behaviorist at the SC Aquarium, and
Rico Walder, Assistant Curator of Forests, Tennessee Aquarium
Beavers: Kathryn Dudeck, Wildlife Director at Chattahoochee Nature Center
Boto (Amazon) Dolphins: Tamara Mcguire, PhD, Amazon Researcher with Virtual Explorers
Indus River Dolphin & Boto Dolphin: Frazer McGilvray, Senior Manager at Conservation International
Capybaras: Rachael Macy, Zoological Manager/Carnivores at the St. Louis Zoo
Water Voles: Rob Strachan, of The Mammal Society (UK)
Mink: George Shurvington, Wildlife Biologist, and Karen Armstrong, Conservation Education
Consultant at the Missouri Department of Conservation
Asian Short-Clawed Otter: Lisa Smith, Curator of Large Mammals at Zoo Atlanta
Hippos: Loran Wlodarski, Science Writer, SeaWorld Orlando
Platypus: Geoff Williams, Australian Platypus Conservancy

All over the world, mammals burrow in snug dens or snooze on riverbeds of sand and silt. While these animals rest, the water sings a burbling lullaby as it laps against the bank.
What would it be like to dream by a stream?

Beside a stream that flows into the Mississippi River, two young otters slip inside a hollow tree.

With the help of their mother, the youngsters rub and nuzzle until their fur is dry and clean. One young otter pokes the other and starts a game of chase. They play until at last they're tuckered out. Then they all lump up together for a long, leisurely snooze.

In a creek near the St. Lawrence River, a beaver family has built a snug lodge. At bedtime, a beaver swims to an underwater doorway and crawls up a tunnel into a dark den.

After grooming every droplet of water off its dense coat, the beaver hunkers down.

It tucks its head between its hind legs and hugs front paws to its chest. In a dry furry heap, the beaver falls sound asleep.

The mighty Amazon River rushes through rainforest and grassland. Pink river dolphins, called botos, live in the Amazon's waters. During rainy season, when the river overflows onto the grasslands, a tired boto searches for a shallow spot. There, it swims lazily near the surface. Rising and breathing, sinking and sleeping, the boto rests in rich, dark water.

Nearby, a capybara, the world's biggest rodent, lumbers along a slow-moving stream.

On a flattened mat of grass, the capybara stretches its stubby front feet and yawns, showing its big teeth.

With a belly full of swamp plants, it tucks in its feet and clicks with contentment. The soft swish of the slow stream soothes the capybara to sleep.

Along the bank of the Thames River, a water vole nibbles on tender reeds. Splashing into the muddy water, the vole slips inside the underwater entrance of her den.

Up in a warm, dry room, her tiny babies start to stir. The mother vole dries her chestnut fur as the babies nuzzle close and nurse. Nestled together on a bed of dried grasses, the vole family falls fast asleep.

On a frosty morning, a mink dives below the ice of the Danube River. It catches a fish and carries it to a makeshift burrow beneath the roots of a tree. Alone and snug, the mink enjoys a morning meal. Then it fluffs its rich, cocoa-brown fur before a day-long snooze. When twilight comes, the mink will awaken to hunt again. It may travel miles downstream. Perhaps the mink will find a cozy den that once belonged to a water vole for tomorrow's snooze.

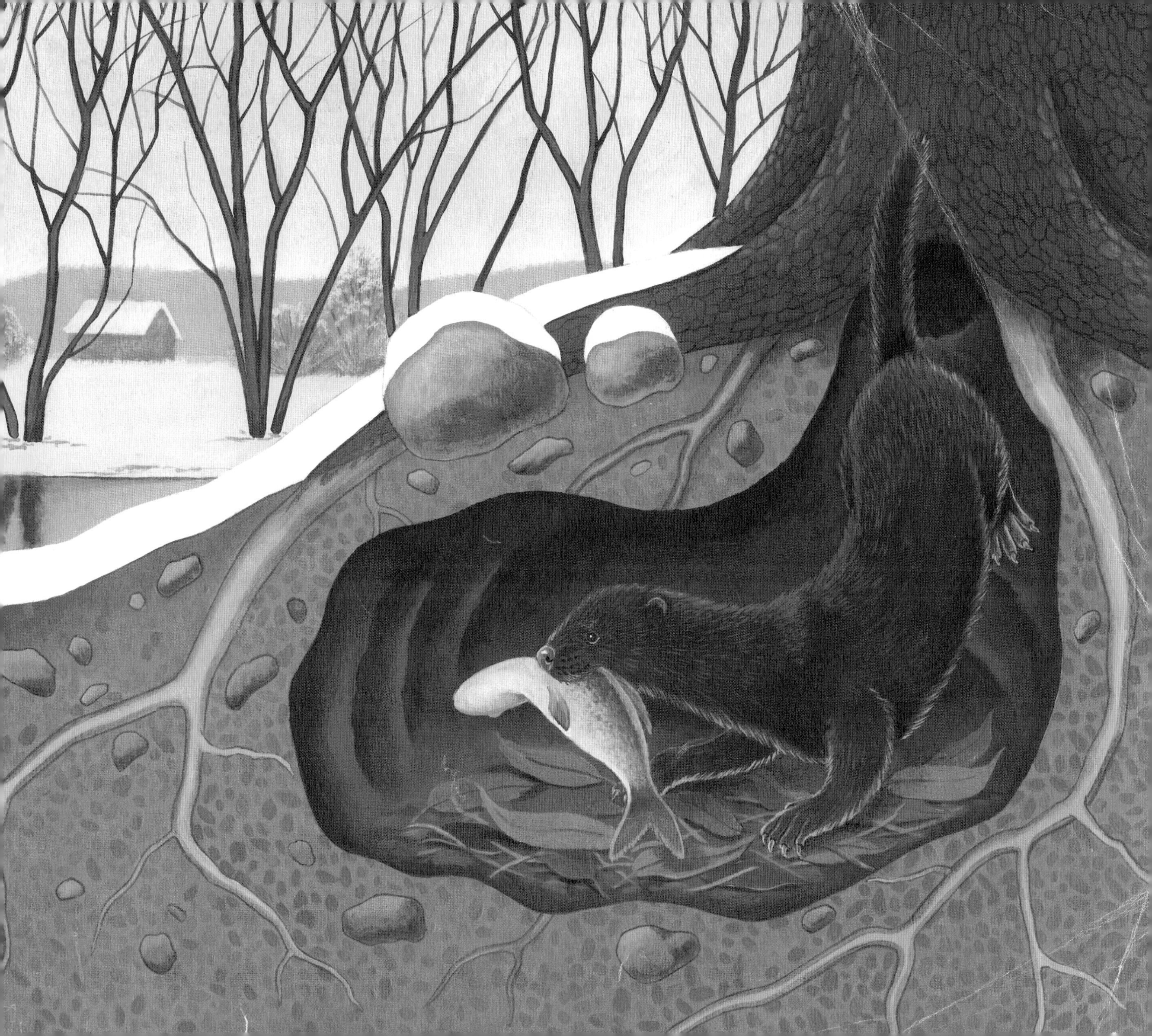

Below the swift,
muddy water of the
Indus River, sunlight
looks like a shimmer
of golden purple.
A river dolphin
listens for the echo of
its staccato clicks as
it swims on its side,
touching the river
bottom with its flipper.

Once a minute, the dolphin rises to the surface to breathe. Day and night, this nearly-blind dolphin swims, napping for mere seconds before it wakes to click and touch and breathe again.

An Asian short-clawed otter, the smallest type of otter in the world, follows its family into a den near the mouth of the Mekong River.

The little otter nibbles every drop of water out of its velvety fur, then wiggles around to dry itself in the dirt.

One by one, all the otters curl up close and cozy. Letting its head droop on a neighbor's warm rump, the little otter's whiskers twitch as it sleeps.

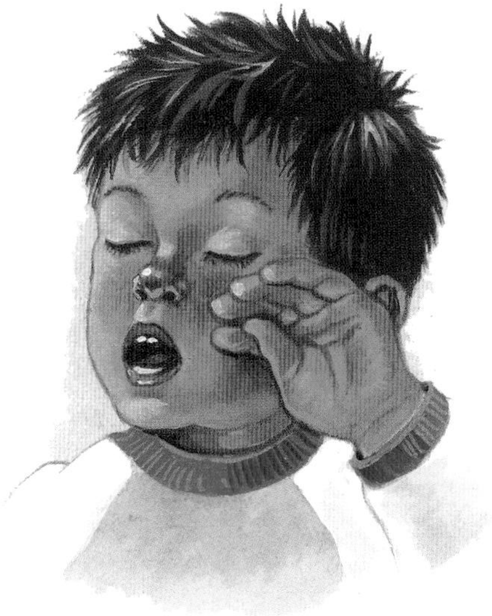

A herd of hippos bounces along the Nile River. Their round backs reflect the strong sunlight like gray boulders poking above the water.

Insects drone in the hot air and buzz around a hippo's ears.

One of the hippos lowers its big face into the cool liquid. Its heavy head rests on a soft pillow of water as it slumbers under the hot African sun.

A wet platypus pops into a hole in the bank of the Brisbane River. As it waddles through the narrow tunnel, the soil sponges water off its thick, glossy fur. Deep inside a dark, quiet den, it lays its ducky beak on soft earth. The platypus shuts its beady eyes and sinks into a long, lazy sleep of river dreams.

It's fun to imagine a snooze by a stream. But a warm, cozy bed is the perfect spot for a human mammal to rest. There's plenty of space in your sleeping den, little person, so stretch out and give a great big yawn. Curl up on a soft pillow, burrow under dry covers, and close your eyes. Let the rhythmic lap, lap of water lull you to sleep as you drift downstream, dreaming of rivers far and near.

For Creative Minds

All of the animals in this book are mammals, like us. Mammals are usually born alive and their babies drink milk from their mothers. Mammals have hair or fur, breathe air, and are warm blooded.

Adaptation Matching Activity

All animals have behavioral or physical traits that help them adapt to their environment. See if you can match the adaptations and descriptions to the animal:

1. ____

2. ____

3. ____

4. ____

a. Asian Short-Clawed Otter:
The smallest of all otters, they have webbed paws with short, blunt claws used for swimming and grabbing prey. They use about 12 different calls to communicate with one another.

b. Platypus:
The duck-like bill is both a nose and a mouth and is packed with thousands of sensors to help find food. Their front feet are webbed like a duck's and their toes stretch into "paddles."

c. Boto Dolphin:
Their long beaks have sharp teeth to grab and hold onto fish and bristly hairs to "touch" things. They can turn their necks so they can look 90 degrees in any direction. These animals are endangered.

d. Capybara:
These large rodents have eyes and ears close to the top of their heads so they can see and hear while swimming. They have four toes and some webbing on their front feet.

e. Hippopotamus:

These large animals have their eyes, ears, and nostrils high on their heads so they can stay in the water most of the day. Their pink sweat helps to protect their skin—kind of like a sunscreen!

f. Indus River Dolphin:

Almost blind, these animals don't use their eyes to see in the dark river water, but they use a special type of hearing called echolocation. These animals are endangered and it is estimated that there are less than 1000 left.

g. Mink:

Their thick, water-repellant fur keeps them warm in cold weather. They use their partly-webbed feet to hunt underwater prey. They are about the size of a house cat.

h. Beaver:

They use their long, thick tails to help steer in the water and to slap the water to warn others of danger. Tails can grow to 10 - 16 inches long and can be 5 - 6 inches wide.

i. River Otter:

Their webbed feet with claws help them to swim and to climb onto land. Their very thick fur keeps them warm in cold water. They have as many hairs in a single square inch as most people have on their whole heads!

j. Water Vole:

Sometimes confused with brown rats, these animals live on river banks and are very territorial. They'll mark the outside of their territory by urinating.

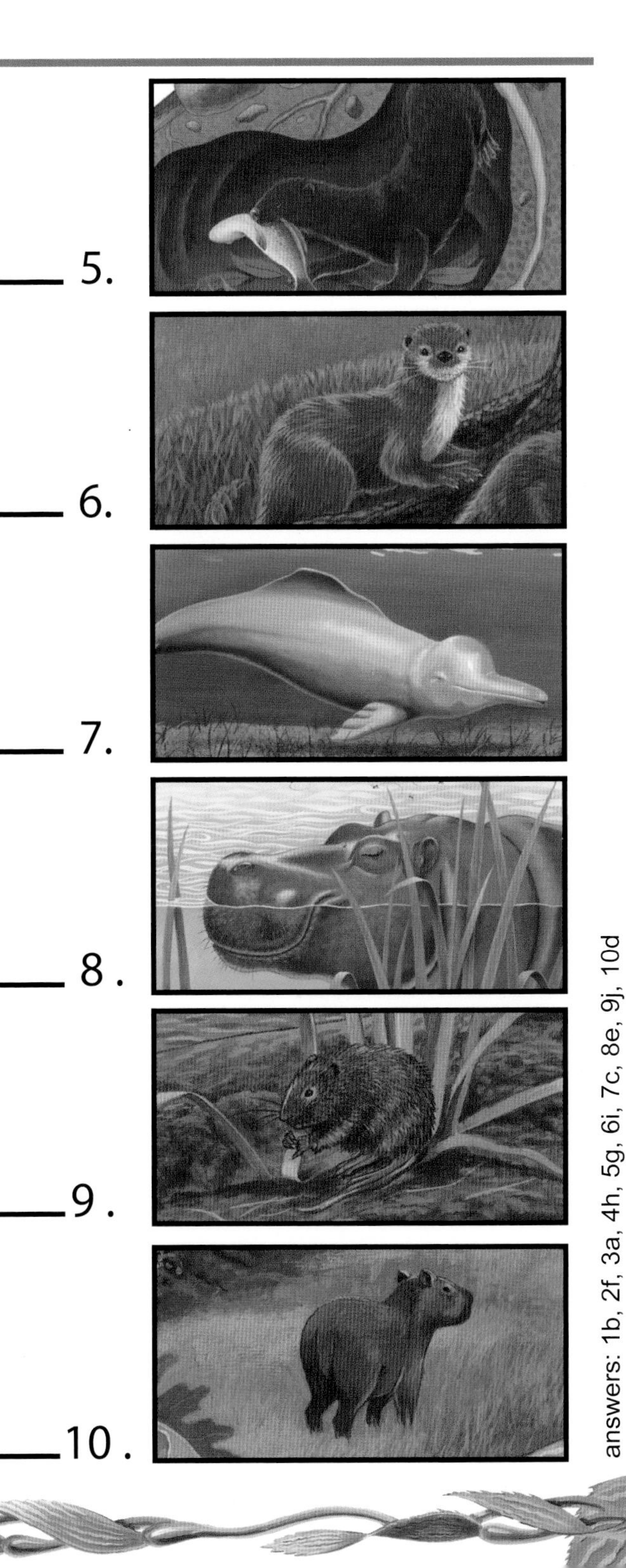

_____ 5.

_____ 6.

_____ 7.

_____ 8.

_____ 9.

_____ 10.

answers: 1b, 2f, 3a, 4h, 5g, 6i, 7c, 8e, 9j, 10d

River Map Activity

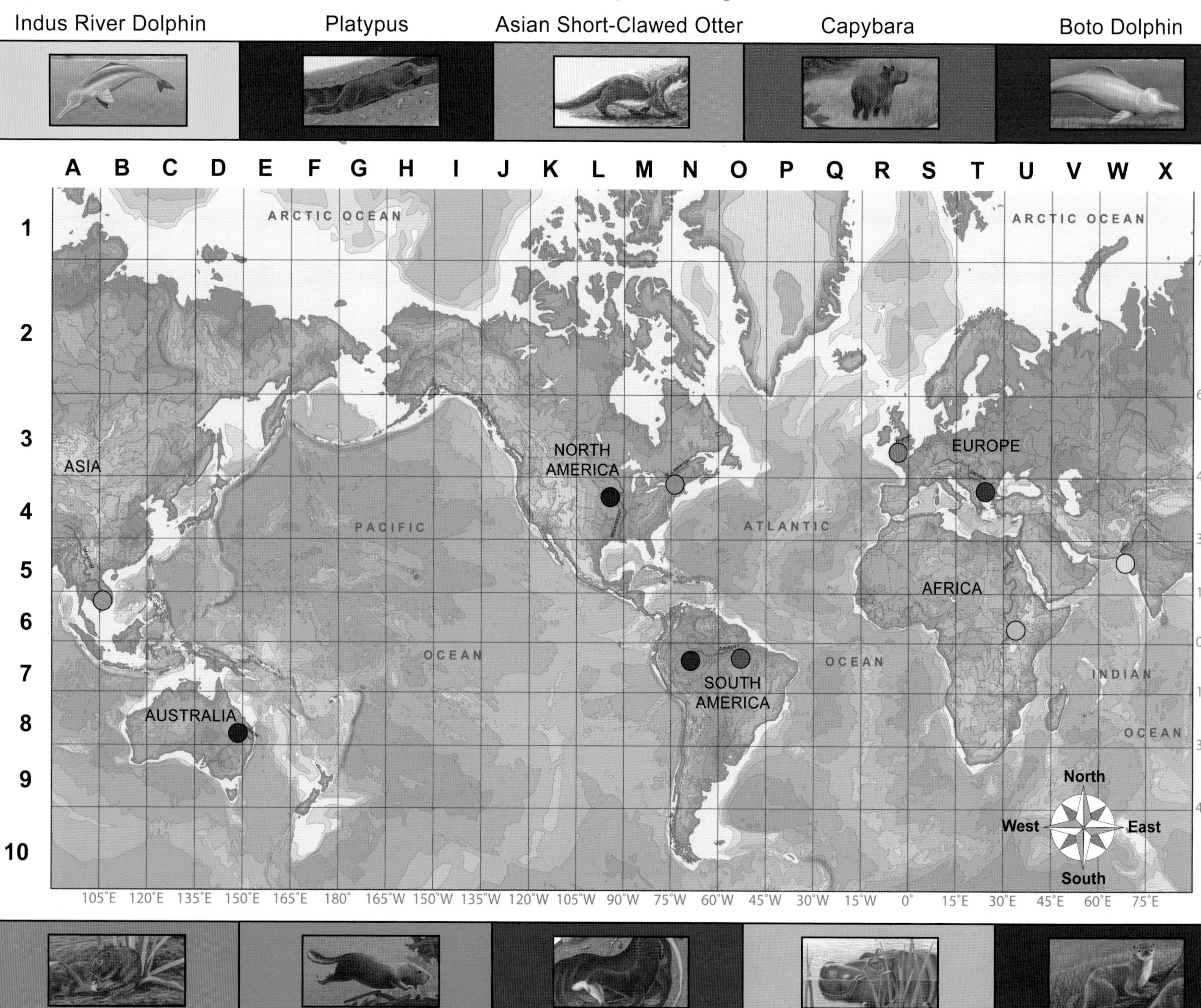
Indus River Dolphin
Platypus
Asian Short-Clawed Otter
Capybara
Boto Dolphin
A B C D E F G H I J K L M N O P Q R S T U V W X
1 2 3 4 5 6 7 8 9 10
ARCTIC OCEAN
ARCTIC OCEAN
ASIA
NORTH AMERICA
EUROPE
PACIFIC
ATLANTIC
AFRICA
OCEAN
OCEAN
INDIAN
OCEAN
SOUTH AMERICA
AUSTRALIA
North
West
East
South
105°E 120°E 135°E 150°E 165°E 180° 165°W 150°W 135°W 120°W 105°W 90°W 75°W 60°W 45°W 30°W 15°W 0° 15°E 30°E 45°E 60°E 75°E
Water Vole
Beaver
Mink
Hippopotamus
River Otter

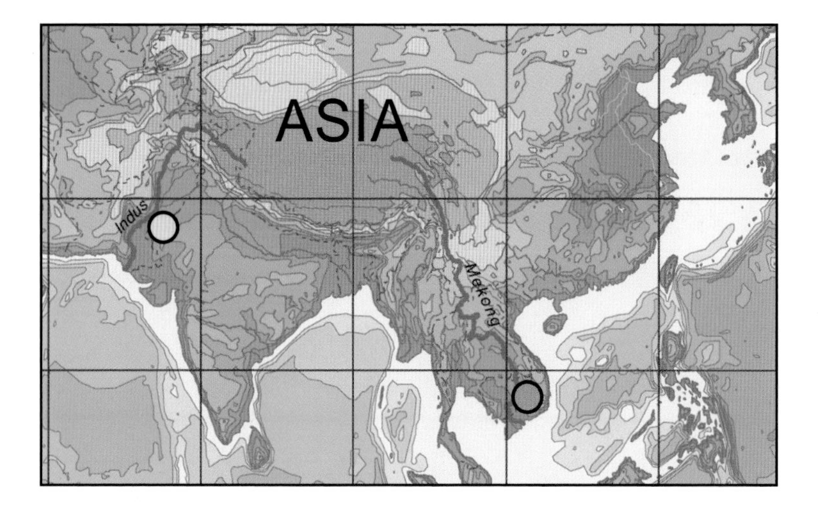
ASIA
Indus
Mekong

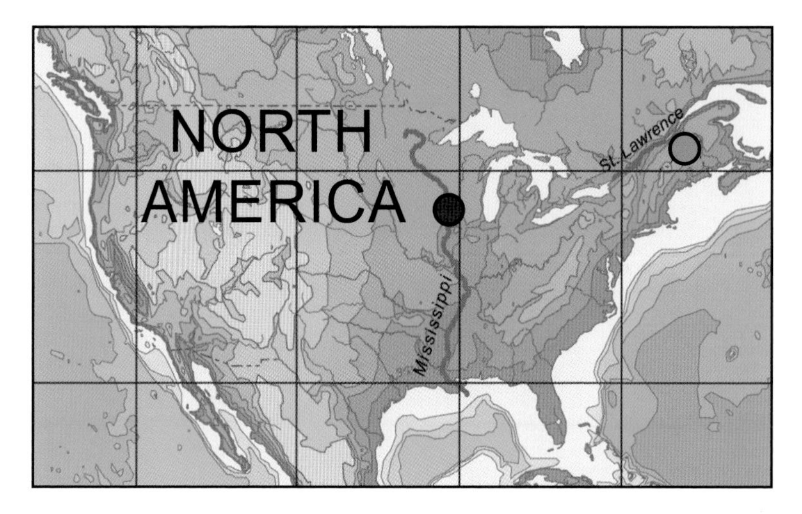
NORTH AMERICA
St. Lawrence
Mississippi

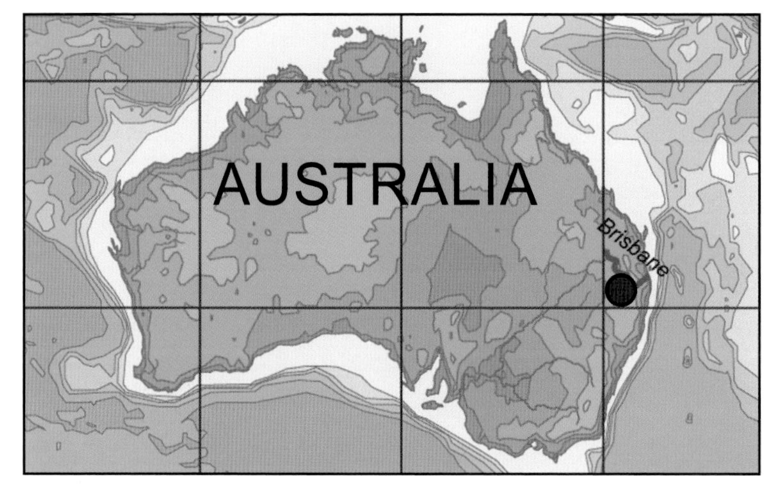
AUSTRALIA
Brisbane

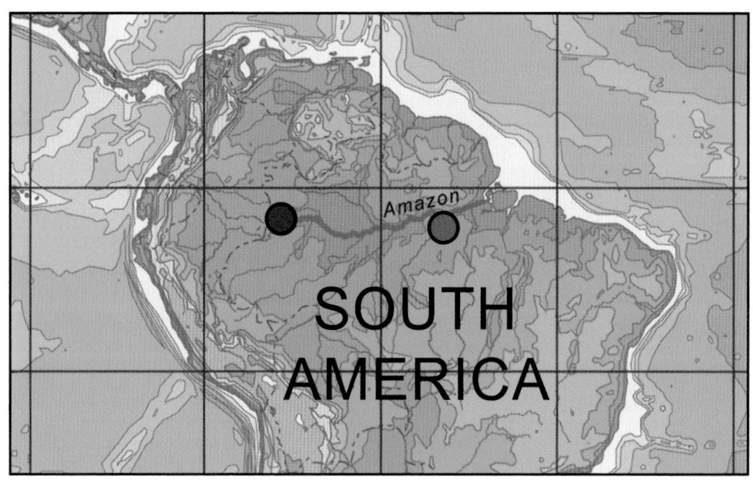
Amazon
SOUTH AMERICA

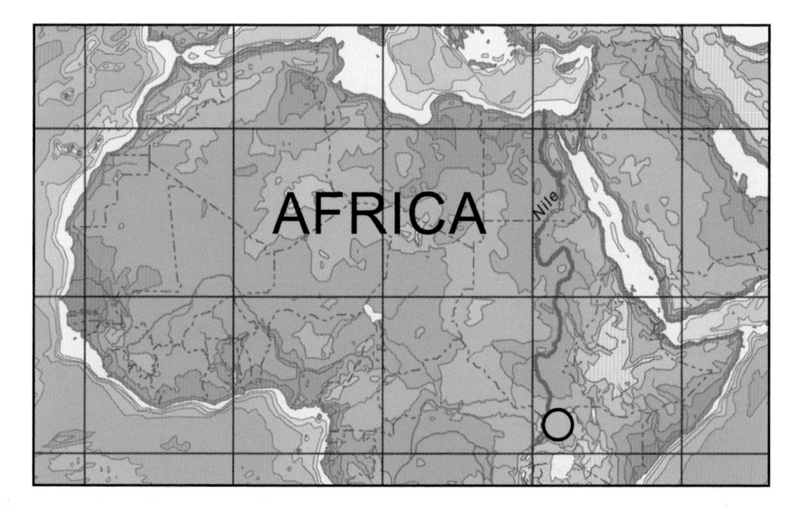
AFRICA
Nile

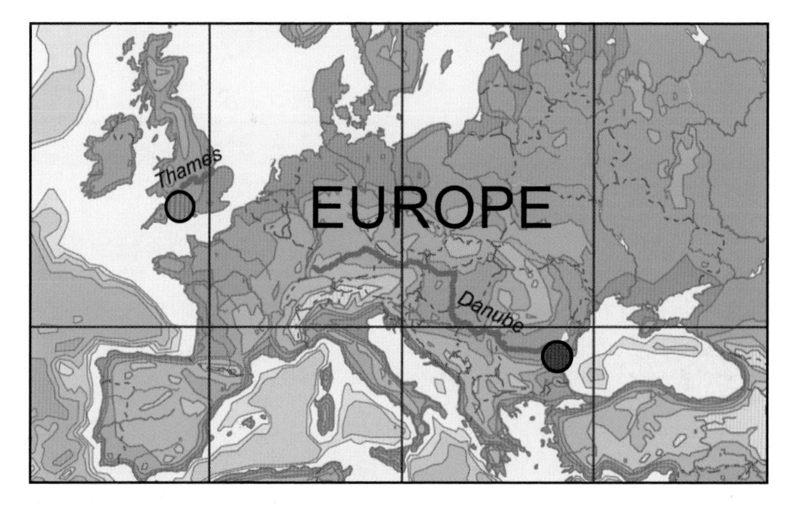
Thames
EUROPE
Danube

Find the animals and their rivers on the map

For young children: Each animal has a colored rectangle around it that matches a similarly-colored dot on the map.

- Match the colors to find the river where each animal lives.
- On what continent are the rivers and animals found?
- On what continent do you live?
- What animal(s) in the book live(s) on the same continent as you do?
- Can you point to where you live on the map?

For older children: Use the coordinate grids (top and left of the map) or the lines of latitude (on the right) and longitude (on the bottom) to answer the questions below. Answers are upside down on the bottom of the page.

1. What animal is found in grid (R,3)?
2. Which other animal is found in Europe?
3. Which animal is found in Australia and at what grid coordinates?
4. Which South American animals live close to the equator (latitude 0º).
5. What animal is found in grid (U,6)?
6. The dot for the beaver is on what line of latitude?
7. What animal is found in grid (L,4)?

Answers: 1) water vole, 2) mink, 3) platypus at (D,8) or approximately 30º south latitude, 150º east longitude; 4) boto dolphin and capybara, 5) hippopotamus, 6) 45º north latitude, 7. river otter.